STORM CATS

written by Malachy Doyle
illustrated by Stuart Trotter

To Celeste, Bracken and Milo
M.D.

For Vicki, Lily, Edward and Tilly
S.T.

SIMON AND SCHUSTER
First published in Great Britain in 2002 by Simon & Schuster UK Ltd
Africa House, 64-78 Kingsway, London WC2B 6AH.
This paperback edition published in 2004.

Text copyright © 2002 Malachy Doyle.
Illustrations copyright © 2002 Stuart Trotter.

ISBN 0-689-86116-8
Printed in China
1 3 5 7 9 10 8 6 4 2

She was a cat,

and he was a cat,

and no, never once did they meet.

For he lived in her house,
and she lived in his,

on opposite sides of the street.

She walked on her side,

and he walked on his,

and that is how things would have stayed.

But for one winter night,
when nothing felt right,
and the two little cats were afraid

A terrible storm
hit the city that night,

and both of them ran off to hide.

But the wind felled a tree,
and it slammed the hole shut

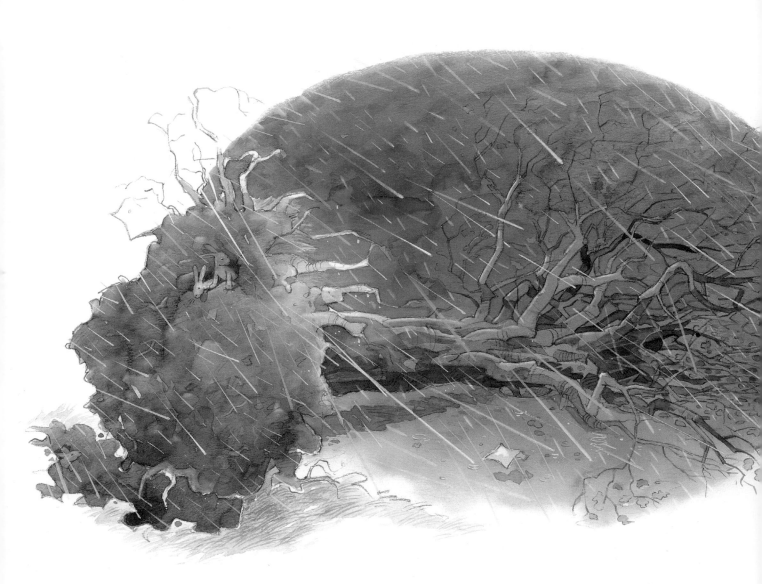

leaving two frightened cats trapped inside.

Now he was a boy,

and she was a girl,

and no, never once did they meet.

For she lived in her house,
and he lived in his,

on opposite sides of the street.

He played with his friends,

and she played with hers,

each, you could say, was a stranger.

And that night they both slept

in their separate rooms,

unaware that their pets were in danger.

The morning brought worry
and sadness and tears,

for neither child's cat could be found.

Oh, have you seen Miro?

And have you seen Ben?
Oh, surely, you've seen him around?

So together they searched,

high and low,

far and wide,

both crying out for their pet.

Oh, look, I've found Miro!
And look, I've found Ben!
They're fine! And they're not even wet!

Now Miro's had kittens,
and Ben is the dad,
and everyone's gathered together.
They've all come around,
to admire the result . . .

of the night of the terrible weather.